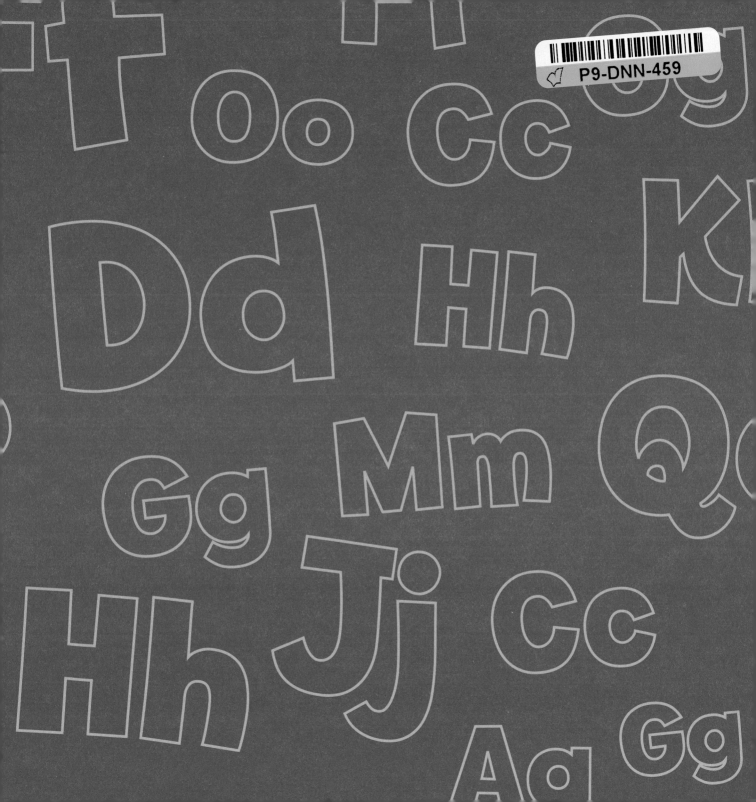

O is for Oregon

written by kids for kids

A is for Aquarium

Sharks and rays
circling the glass,
Stare at me
as I walk past.

B

is for **Beaver**

Looks like a beaver
chewed this wood.
He thinks that
it tastes very good.

C

is for **Crater Lake**

After Mount Mazama blew its top,
The hole was filled drop by drop.

D

is for

Duck

Portland is a puddle town,
Where ducks feel at home
waddling around.

E

is for Evergreen

The trees in Oregon are always green.
They keep our air and rivers clean.

F is for **Farm**

Way, way out in the green country
Are farms that feed us and keep us healthy.

G

is for **Gorge**

High rocky cliffs
carved by the river.
Just looking at them
makes me shiver.

H is for **Mount Hood**

Sledding, skiing, and snowboarding, too,
On the clean white snow, under the sky so blue.

Indigenous People

The Chinook, Paiute, and Klamath are here,
Plus many more Oregon tribes live near.

J

is for

Japanese Garden

Konichiwa! The Garden welcomes you.
See the iris, the koi ponds, and the bamboo.

K

is for **Kite**

Soaring in the turquoise sky,
Colorful like a butterfly.

L is for **Lewis and Clark**

They explored this place, with Sacagawea, too,
To find a route to the Pacific, our ocean big and blue.

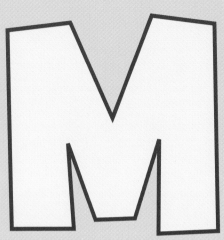

M

is for

Multnomah Falls

Water rushing from
cliffs so high,
Pouring down from
that beautiful sky.

N is for
Neahkahnie Mountain
Ships with black flags, hooks for hands,
Buried their treasure on this mountainous land.

O

is for **Oregon Trail**

Fathers, daughters, sons, and wives
Going west to make new lives.

P is for Pendleton Round-Up

Buck me once. Buck me twice.

But buck me three times? That's not very nice.

Q is for

Rose Festival Queen

Bands and floats move down the street,
But the Queen is the one we want to meet.

R

is for

Rose City

When in Portland,
there are so many
things to do:
Drink some coffee,
read a book, maybe
take a walk or two.

S

is for

Salmon

Swimming, splashing
from river to sea,
Following the path of
their ancestry.

T is for

Tillamook

Tillamook cheese
is very nice.
I wonder if
I can have a slice?

U is for **Umbrella**

In Oregon if you are without an umbrella
You are one unlucky fella!

V is for

Vineyard

Our wine is tasty,
white or red.
But my mom says
sometimes it goes to
her head.

W

is for
Whale

Whales pass through;
they spout their water blue,
And sometimes you can
see them, too.

X is for

eXtreme Sports

Here in Oregon extreme sports thrive. You can windsurf, mountain bike, snowboard, and skydive.

 is for

Yaquina Head Lighthouse

On top of the lighthouse,
over the sea,
That is where I want to be.

Z

is for **Zoo**

Tigers, giraffes,
and elephants, too.
Come see all the animals
at the Oregon Zoo.

Oh My Gosh!

Aquarium
There are more than 500 species of animals at the Oregon Coast Aquarium, including 21 kinds of sea stars, helping make it one of the top 10 aquariums in the country.

Beaver
The biggest beaver dam ever was 2,140 feet long! There are so many beavers in Oregon, the animal is even a school mascot. Chew on, Oregon State Beavers!

Crater Lake
Crater Lake is filled with approximately 4.6 trillion gallons of water from rainfall and snowmelt. It is the seventh-deepest lake in the world and the deepest in the country at 1,932 feet.

Duck
Ducks feel right at home in Oregon because of all our rain. We even have a school with a duck mascot: the University of Oregon Ducks. Go Ducks!

Evergreen
The largest tree in Oregon was a 216-foot Sitka spruce. It lived 750 years—that means it was already 500 years old when the U.S. was founded! It was also the largest Sitka spruce in the country until a lightning bolt and windstorm killed it in 2007.

Farm
Oregon farms produce the most peppermint, hazelnuts, blackberries, and Christmas trees in the United States.

The Gorge
The long Gorge valley acts like a wind tunnel. Multiple times a year the winds reach almost 70 miles an hour. That's as fast as all those cars flying by on the highway!

Mount Hood
Mount Hood stands 11,249 feet high and is the only place in the lower 48 states where you can ski year-round.

Indigenous People
While there are only 10 official Native American tribes in Oregon today, there used to be more than 50 including the Tillamook and Multnomah.

Japanese Garden
Portland's Japanese Garden is one of 60 similar gardens in the United States. It is made up of five different garden styles: the Flat Garden, the Tea Garden, the Natural Garden, the Strolling Pond Garden, and the Sand and Stone Garden.

Facts about the

Kite

Every year the Summer Kite Festival is held on the beach in Lincoln City, Oregon, which is considered one of the best places to fly kites in North America. The most kites flown in the sky at one time is 4,663.

Lewis & Clark

In 1803, Meriwether Lewis and William Clark led the first overland journey across the U.S. They walked, paddled, and rode horses nearly 4,000 miles from St. Louis, Missouri, to the Pacific Ocean. The trip took a year and a half, and then they spent four *more* rainy months at Fort Clatsop, Oregon, near the mouth of the Columbia River, before returning east.

Multnomah Falls

With water spilling down 620 feet, Multnomah Falls is the highest waterfall in the state and the second highest in the nation. It is one of more than 400 waterfalls in Oregon.

Neahkahnie Mountain

This mountain may be the home of hidden treasure. Legends say 500 years ago sailors from a Spanish galleon buried a chest of gold there. It's supposed to be marked by a carved rock and guarded by a ghost. The treasure has yet to be found . . .

Oregon Trail

The Oregon Trail was 2,170 miles long, carrying 52,000 immigrants to Oregon from 1840 to 1859. As pioneers made their way across the Great Plains, they noticed that the Oregon Trail was covered with buffalo poop. The resourceful pioneers used the dried dung to make fires and the kids used them as Frisbees!

Pendleton Round-Up

The first unofficial Round-Up was on July 4, 1909. It included bronc riding, horse races by Indians and non-Indians, Indian feasts and war dances, greased pig contests, sack races, foot races, and fireworks. Today some 50,000 people come to Pendleton to see the show!

Rose Festival Queen

At first the Rose Queen was selected from Portland debutantes. But since 1931 Portland school students have been electing the Rose Festival Queen based on her school and volunteer activities. They have elected some amazing girls, including four girls named Dorothy! Click those ruby slippers and head to the Rose Parade!

great state of Oregon

Rose City

Portland is known as the "Rose City" because our climate is perfect for growing them. Portland is also home to the International Rose Test Garden, where they create new kinds of roses every year. During World War I, rose growers in Europe sent their roses to the garden to keep them from being destroyed in the bombings.

Salmon

Oregon is home to four different species of salmon: chum, coho, steelhead, and the biggest one that can weigh up to 100 pounds, chinook salmon.

Tillamook

The cheese makers at Tillamook have been using the same recipe for their delicious cheese for 100 years! It has never changed. They produce 160,000 pounds of cheese and 8,000 gallons of ice cream per day!

Umbrella

The average rainfall in Oregon ranges from less than 8 inches in the drier areas to 200 inches in the mountains. Those folks need an umbrella!

Vineyard

Oregon has over 350 wineries growing 72 different kinds of grapes. Oregon's #1 wine is Pinot Noir (pronounced *peeno-nwa*).

Whale

Each year about 18,000 gray whales migrate past the Oregon coast from mid-December to mid-January. They are on their way south to Mexico to give birth to their young. When they pass by again from March through June on their way north, the calves travel in front of the adults. Other whales you might see are the sperm, orca, minke, humpback, and blue whales.

eXtremes Sports

In Oregon you can go hang gliding, skydiving, mountain biking, rock and mountain climbing, kayaking, windsurfing, kite- and wakeboarding. Oregonians are always inventing new ways to go to the eXtreme!

Yaquina Head Lighthouse

The light of this 136-year-old lighthouse continues to shine helping ships with navigation. At 162 feet above sea level, it is the tallest lighthouse on the Oregon coast.

Zoo

The Oregon Zoo is the home of the largest and oldest Asian elephant born in a zoo in North America. His name is Packy and he has been the father of seven calves during his record-breaking lifetime.

Thanks to the amazing teachers
at Winterhaven School for encouraging
your students and their creativity!
Thanks to Patty Jensen, principal
Tanya Ghattas, and Lisa Abramovic for
your support and enthusiasm for this project.
And thanks to Whitney Quon . . . for everything!
But most of all, thanks to the Winterhaven
students who wrote such fantastic poetry
for this book. Way to go!

Photo by Jennifer Jones

Keely Abramovic-Doane (M)
Julian Andrews (S)
Asher Jacob Antoine
Abe Asher
Merriel Ater
Caroline Baber
Shayla Bailey
Madeleine Banks
Cleo Bethel
Flannery Bethel
Zoe Bluffstone
Max Boyd
Alexander Brown
Cory Brown
Jessica Brown
Katy Brown

Sophie Brown
Elise Brunk
Michael Burke
Peyton Butsch (H)
Allison Carpenter
Miette Clearman (C)
Seneca Clemons
Alexander Coffin
Ilana Cohen
Alexander Cummings
Dominic de Bettencourt
Sequoya de Nevers
Luci Doherty
Sam Dornfest
Miles Drake
Raisa Ebner (O)

Davis Einolf
Devon Essick
Eleanor Ewing
Madeleine Fall
Emilie Fisher
Maria Rowen Flores (T)
Tuesday Foust (Y)
Gwen Frost
Hallie Frost (N)
Hannah Fuller (Q)
Josh Gillis
Mira Hanfling
Elizabeth Harding
Autumn Jernigan
Sabrina Jernigan
Emma Jones

Erika Karlin
Hattie Kirby (W)
Cholame Kofard
Noah Kruss (P & V)
Tova Kruss (P & V)
Andrew Laurila
Owen Lowe-Rogstad (E)
Kelsey McCall
Ronan McCann (A)
Aesha Mokashi (K)
Adam Nayak
Esther Nita
Anna Notti (F)
Zachary Notti (G)
Ruby O'Connor
Hannah Parker

Anna Peterson
Alana Rivas-Scott (Z)
Margaret Rose (U)
Sophia Sahm (Z)
Douglas Sam (X)
Alex Steiner (J)
Hugh Steiner
Leo Steiner (L)
Libby Steiner (R)
Finn Vega (D)
Georgia Welch
Hannah Welsh
Andy Yu
Vivian Yu
William Yu
Brett Zonick (B)

Text © 2008 by WestWinds Press®

The following photographers hold copyright to their images as indicated: John Marshall, **O**; Rick Schafer, **I, L, P, T**; William Sullivan, **N**; Cindy Hanson/Oregon Coast Aquarium, **A**; DanitaDelimont.com: Jerry and Marcy Monkman, **B**; Janis Miglavs, **C**, **Q, R, Y, Z**; Scott Batchelar, **E/front cover top**; David R. Frazier, **F**; Stephen Datnoff, **H**; Mark Downey, **J**; Bill Bachmann, **K**; Jamie and Judy Wild, **M**; Paul Souders, **S, W**; Luckylook, **U/back cover**; Lee Klopfer, **X**; IndexOpen.com: ImageDJ, **D**; FogStock LLC, **G, V, front cover bottom**.

Fourth printing 2010

Library of Congress Cataloging-in-Publication Data
O is for Oregon.
    p. cm.
 ISBN 978-0-88240-747-0 (hardbound)
1. Oregon—Juvenile literature. 2. Alphabet books—Juvenile literature.
 F876.3.O23 2008
 979.5—dc22

                 2008009591

WestWinds Press®
An imprint of Graphic Arts Books
P.O. Box 56118
Portland, OR 97238-6118
(503) 254-5591

Editor: Michelle McCann
Designer: Vicki Knapton

PP/Logan, Iowa, USA
12/10, 352649